Gwenda & the Animals

TESSA DAHL

Gwenda & the Animals

ILLUSTRATED BY
ANTHONY CARNABUCI

VIKING

VIKING
Published by the Penguin Group
Viking Penguin, a division of Penguin Books USA Inc.,
375 Hudson Street, New York, New York 10014, U.S.A.
Penguin Books Ltd, 27 Wrights Lane, London W8 5TZ, England
Penguin Books Australia Ltd, Ringwood, Victoria, Australia
Penguin Books Canada Ltd, 2801 John Street, Markham, Ontario, Canada L3R 1B4
Penguin Books (N.Z.) Ltd, 182–190 Wairau Road, Auckland 10, New Zealand

Penguin Books Ltd, Registered Offices: Harmondsworth, Middlesex, England

First published in Great Britain by Hamish Hamilton Ltd, 1989
First American edition with new illustrations published in 1990
1   3   5   7   9   10   8   6   4   2
Text copyright © Tessa Dahl, 1989
Illustrations copyright © Anthony Carnabuci, 1990
All rights reserved

Library of Congress Cataloging in Publication Data
Dahl, Tessa.   Gwenda and the animals by Tessa Dahl;
illustrated by Anthony Carnabuci.—1st American ed.   p.   cm.
Summary: Having had a horrible first visit to the zoo, Gwenda stays after
hours and transforms it into a happier place for all the animals.
ISBN 0-670-83020-8   [1. Zoos—Fiction. 2. Zoo animals—Fiction.]
I. Carnabuci, Anthony, il. II. Title.
PZ7.D15154Gw 1990   [E]—dc20   90-32599   CIP   AC

Printed in Japan
Set in Garamond #3

TO MY GODCHILDREN
(in order of appearance)

Emma Pearl
Matthew Spalding
Doune Couper
Kate Powell
Nicholas Schilcher
Jack Burns
Annelie Fawke
Jake Thomson
Lukas Previn
Thomas Adeane
Thomas Sturridge
Poppy Delevigne
Theo Brown
Tamsin Vaughan
Fred Farrell
Maisie McNeice
Jo Padfield

WITH ALL MY LOVE
T.D.

CONTENTS

Gwenda & the Animals

Revolting Uncle Matt

Gwenda, her mother, her twin baby brothers Paul and Tom, her Auntie Rosie, Uncle Matt, her cousins Amy, Beth, Sarah, and Ross, all went to the zoo for the day. It was wet. It was chaos. Gwenda was not happy. Her Uncle Matt was being really stupid and teasing the animals. The others thought it was funny. Gwenda did not.

At the penguin pool, Uncle Matt waddled around and the other children followed.

"What twerps," thought Gwenda.

At the sea lions, he barked and clapped his hands like flippers, and the others did it, too.

"More like sea morons," said Gwenda to herself.

In the monkey house, Uncle Matt pretended to swing around with Ross on his back. The others scratched under their arms and screeched and squealed. The monkeys looked disgusted.

Gwenda felt disgusted. She looked at the mother monkey and whispered, "I'm sorry, I'm so sorry."

As she turned to leave, she heard someone say in a hushed voice, "That's all right, we're used to it."

I must be hearing things, she thought. The others clearly hadn't noticed anything as they lumbered around looking goofy.

In the lions' cage, the lioness paced up and down. Up and down, up and down.

Uncle Matt copied her. So did Amy, Beth, Sarah, and Ross. Auntie Rosie and Mom laughed. The lion yawned and watched them crossly.

"Stupid idiots," Gwenda heard a deep voice mutter.

She looked around. There was no one else nearby.

The panda bears were no better. One lay curled up on the ground and the other sat swaying to and fro.

"Hey, black eyes!" yelled Uncle Matt, "been in a fight? Wannanother one?"

He rolled up his sleeves and started to poke a long stick into the cage.

Gwenda could stand it no more. "Uncle Matt, stop it. Stop teasing the animals. They're stuck in cages and you're being stupid and cruel."

Uncle Matt swung around, furious. His face had gone purple.

"Now don't you talk to your Uncle Matt like that," said Gwenda's mother. "He's older and wiser than you."

As they turned to leave Gwenda heard a little whisper.

"Older yes, wiser, oh, no." Then a laugh.

She ran back to the cage. "Was that you?" she asked. "Was that really you?"

"No," said the panda. "Dumb animals can't talk."

Gwenda began to tingle. Her head felt fuzzy, as if she had hundreds of silver fish swimming inside her brain. She felt as if a dolphin was diving in her tummy. Her insides were tumbling. It was a glorious, exciting feeling, like a Roman candle firework shooting out sparkles which zinged down her body and rolled to her toes. She knew these were magical happenings, and best of all, she felt like she had a wonderful, beautiful bird

in her chest, flapping its wings and singing.

When they arrived at the parking lot, her mother was busy putting away the stroller and strapping the twins into their seats, while Uncle Matt loaded the other children into his car.

"Mom," she said, "I'm going home with the others, okay?"

Gwenda's mother didn't look up. "All right, I'll see you around six. Don't be late."

Gwenda darted behind the parked cars. She watched Uncle Matt drive off, his car full of laughing, dirty faces.

Then she watched her mother go.

Well, Gwenda, you've done it now, she said to herself.

Gwenda and the Pandas

Gwenda was nimble. It was easy to duck past the ticket collector and under the turnstile.

The last of the visitors were milling around and she joined them, edging her way slowly back to the pandas.

When she was nearly at their cage, she took a deep breath and jumped into a rubbish bin. It was disgusting and sticky, full of the most revolting smelly things.

Dusk was setting in and she could hear the keepers shouting, "Everyone out. Closing time."

Her bottom was getting wet and slimy. Yuck, thought

9

Gwenda, as she realized she was sitting on a half-eaten chocolate popsicle.

Gwenda waited. The zoo was so noisy she couldn't tell if all the people had gone. It was spooky. Birds were screaming, monkeys were screeching. The lions were roaring and something was growling.

The clatter of the keepers feeding and locking up the animals stopped.

"Good night, Bill, see you tomorrow," she heard.

Slowly Gwenda inched her way out of the bin. She darted across the ground to the pandas' cage. They hadn't gone to bed. The panda that had been curled up was sitting chewing a piece of bamboo shoot and the panda that Gwenda had talked to was watching.

"She's so greedy," he said.

"What?" asked Gwenda.

"You heard me," said the panda in a deep voice, which made Gwenda realize he was the man.

"You said she's greedy."

"You bet she's greedy. She's a greedy pig."

"No, I'm not, I'm a panda," said the other panda, in a squeaky girl's voice.

"Huh, could have fooled me," said the cross male panda.

He moved toward Gwenda and as he did the female

11

panda sighed out loud, "Sticks and stones may break my bones, but words will never hurt me."

"Speaking of sticks," grunted the male panda, "your uncle was revolting today. I couldn't believe you were related to him. But I like you. Most animals—that's what we call humans—laugh at us or poke things through the bars. We're thoroughly disgusted by the way you animals behave."

The female panda was still guzzling.

"You'd better hurry up or she'll eat all your food," warned Gwenda.

"She makes me sick. I'll tell you something. We pandas are from China. I lived a marvelous free life in the hills until I was captured and put in a crate, then onto a plane and brought here. In China I had my choice of wife—now they give me *her* and expect us to get along. How would you like it if you were shoved in a cage and told to fall in love with some boy you'd never met before, especially if you didn't like the look of him?"

"I see your point," said Gwenda, thinking of the most revolting boy in her class. "But you could be nicer to her."

"I just don't like her. We don't get along."

"Have you tried?" asked Gwenda.

"No, he has not," chipped in the female panda. "He's

12

been so unkind to me. I'm homesick and lonely and . . ."

"Are you? You didn't tell me that." The male panda sounded surprised.

"Well, you never asked. In fact, in six months you've hardly spoken to me."

"Is that true?" said Gwenda.

The male panda looked guilty and didn't answer.

"I said is that true?" asked Gwenda in her strictest voice.

"Well, all she does is eat," he grumbled.

"I only eat because I'm bored."

"Look," said Gwenda, "I think you two have a lot of talking to do. No one just gets along. Often you have to work at it. Even people who have been married for years have to try."

"Have a bamboo shoot." The female panda held out her paws.

"Well, I might just do that." He moved a bit closer to her. "I never noticed before, but you've got lovely eyes," he said.

Gwenda smiled, "Good night," she whispered.

"Good night, Gwenda," they answered.

She started to walk away. As she turned the corner she looked back and smiled. The pandas didn't notice.

The Penguins Protest

Gwenda was very happy about the pandas. So she did a little dance. She wasn't worried about her mother or how cross she would be. She wasn't frightened by the dark or the noises. I have magic, she said to herself. Something extraordinary, something peculiar is happening to me. I can help these animals. They are my friends.

She walked past the monkey house. All was quiet. Gwenda knew they had been locked up for the night.

"Sleep well, monkeys," she called, and blew them a kiss.

The penguins were nestling down, getting ready to sleep.

"Hello, boys," said Gwenda.

"Oy, oy, oy. Who have we here?" asked a big penguin. Gwenda realized he was the chief.

"Yes, yes, yes. Who have we here?" echoed the others.

"I'm Gwenda."

"Shouldn't you be at home with your animal relations?" asked the chief.

"I'd rather be here," said Gwenda.

"We wouldn't," said the chief.

"Oh, no, no, no, we wouldn't," said the others. "We come from the beautiful South Pole where we have thousands of miles of icy land to live on, sharp blue sea to swim in, ice hills to slide down, and fresh fish to dive for."

"Fish, fish, fresh fish to dive for," sang the others longingly.

"But we're here and we don't complain. We have no choice."

"No choice, no choice, we have no choice. . . ."

Gwenda noticed how sadly they whispered this.

"But there is one thing that bothers us. It makes us miserable. It fills us with fear."

"What's that?" Gwenda was aching to know.

"Every day at four o'clock we have to do the Penguin Parade. It's stupid, we feel stupid."

"Stupid, stupid, we feel stupid," muttered the others.

"We are marched through the zoo to the pool where we are fed. Everyone laughs at us. People even film us with cameras. No one laughed at us walking in the South Pole. What right have they to laugh, those ugly human animals who are fat or skinny, who have odd shapes and come in different colors? At least we all look the same."

"I agree, it's awful," said Gwenda.

"But that's not it, it's far worse," said the chief.

"Far worse, far worse," nodded the other penguins.

"When we reach the elephants they make us turn right. We hate it. We try and turn left, but they make us turn right. It rattles our bones."

"Rattles our bones, rattles our bones," the penguins said with a shudder.

"But what, what is it, what terrible thing happens if you turn right?"

"Down that path are the wolves," said the chief.

"Aren't they in cages?" asked Gwenda.

"It's not enough."

"Not enough, not enough," the penguins added, shaking their heads.

"Those wolves are evil, bad wolves. They say terrible things to us."

"Like what?" gasped Gwenda.

"Well, as we get closer they start to shout, 'Here comes lunch, penguin burgers, get out the ketchup!' Then they move to the front of their cages, and by the time we get near they are whispering, their horrible sharp teeth shining, 'We're going to get you. We're going to creep out tonight and munch you up. We'll sneak out of our cages, we know where you are, and you won't hear us *until it's too late.*' And then they laugh. Oh, it's horrible, they upset us so much. Can you help us, Gwenda?"

Gwenda thought for a moment. Then her back started to tingle as if a tiny koala bear was crawling up her spine. Suddenly she felt the wonderful, beautiful bird in her chest flapping its wings again.

"Yes, oh, yes," she said. "Of course I can. Good night, penguins, you can sleep well tonight. I'll protect you from the wolves."

Missing Cubs

The light was disappearing. Gwenda knew she did not have much time. Once it was dark the animals would be going to sleep.

Gwenda also knew that her mother would soon be wondering where she was. Then there'd be trouble.

For a moment she felt frightened. Should she stop now and see if she could find a way home? Perhaps she should find a keeper and pretend she'd been left behind.

But then she remembered the animals, her animals, and knew she had to keep going.

Suddenly, as if from nowhere, the bats started to swoop. She watched them shoot through the sky and drop down into the penguin pool, like swallows. Then they would soar up again toward the stars. As she stood trying to make up her mind, a bat skimmed past her head.

"Don't give up, Gwenda," it whispered, and off it sped.

Again, as if a dart had whizzed past her ear, another bat came, getting so close it made her hair rustle.

"Go to the lions, they need you," it squeaked.

"Wait," gasped Gwenda, but the bat had shot into the sky.

Gwenda did not stop to think. She ran. She ran past the sea lions, and as she ran she heard them clapping their flippers and barking, "Go on, Gwenda, go on."

She did not stop. Her feet felt light; her legs seemed to glide. And soon she was right in front of the lions' cage.

"Oh, Gwenda, here you are at last," roared the lion. "Tell us, what does the sign on our cage say?"

Gwenda read the sign on the bars. "It says your cubs can be seen in the children's zoo."

Zelda the lioness started to cry. She roared and shook and sobbed. "They're alive, Zimba. Oh, my darling, they are alive, I knew they were."

Zimba started to lick Zelda's face lovingly.

"It will be all right. Believe me, we'll get them back. Gwenda will help us. Oh, Gwenda, we have had such troubled times. My poor Zelda gave birth to twin cubs a few days ago. We were so happy. We had longed for them. For a day she mothered them, loved them, and fed them. We named them Harry and Mary and we were so proud."

With this Zelda roared again, a sad, empty noise.

Zimba went on: "But the keeper came. He gave us each an injection which put us to sleep. When we woke up, Harry and Mary were gone. Since then our lives have been misery. Zelda has paced up and down, up and down. She will not eat, she will not sleep. She cries for her babies."

"This is terrible," said Gwenda, feeling the tears trickling down her cheeks. "Oh, Zimba, I must help you."

"Not only am I worried about our twins, but I am fearful for Zelda. We come from Kenya, in Africa. We had hundreds of miles of golden land to live on. We were so happy. Zelda and I were free. It was hot and beautiful. It was our kingdom. In Africa, Zelda had many cubs and she was a good mother. But we were captured and put in cages and brought here. We have done our best. We have no

24

choice. We had each other. We have lived behind bars, in the cold. But now we have lost our cubs."

Gwenda shuddered. She tried to imagine how she would feel if someone took her away from her cozy little home and her friends and flew her to a strange country; if she were put into a cage. Even worse, she tried to imagine a person giving her mother an injection and taking away the twins. Gwenda started to get angry. She heard hundreds of bees buzzing in her head. Her fingers started to wriggle like little worms. She felt as if she had a shark in her tummy. Her insides were tumbling with fury, rockets were shooting around her heart.

Gwenda knew she had to help. She realized her magic had been given to her for a reason. It was not for fun. To have this amazing wonderful power was a gift, and now she had to use it. This was serious.

Zimba looked at her. There were tears in his eyes, too. "Gwenda, oh, Gwenda, please help us!"

"I will, oh, yes, I will," she answered.

Gwenda to the Rescue

Bill was not happy. He loved his animals and he was worried. Bill had been head keeper at the zoo for a long time. Things had changed. People seemed to want to be amused by the animals. Bill did not like that. He could remember the days when everyone seemed happy just to admire them. But now that was not enough. Bill knew the animals should not be used to entertain people, but he also knew he had a job to do. He had to keep the crowds coming.

As he made supper that night, in his little cottage by

the zoo gates, he felt sad. Why don't people love the animals? he thought. How can I keep doing this job when I have to keep finding ways to entertain the humans? As he poured himself a mug of tea he thought he saw a little girl walk past his window. Come on, Bill, he said to himself, you're tired, perhaps it's all getting to be too much and you should give up and go and live by the seaside. But then what would happen to your animals? He shuddered. He rubbed his eyes and looked again. No, he wasn't seeing things. Coming up his path there was a little girl.

He heard a knock on the door. Whatever next, thought Bill as he turned the key and opened the door. There stood Gwenda. Bill felt peculiar. He looked at Gwenda. All around her was a huge circle of tiny flames, as if there were hundreds of matches glowing behind her little body. She seemed to be one enormous firework, with beautiful sparks and colored waterfalls shooting out around her. Bill could sense that this tiny person, this small child, was very important. All of a sudden in one enormous rush the tiredness and sadness left him and he started to smile. Then he giggled and the giggling turned to laughter. Gwenda started laughing, too. Then Bill put his hand out and took Gwenda's; and as he touched her he felt a glow,

and a shot of electricity went through him like a bolt of lightning.

They went into his little sitting room. Then Gwenda stopped laughing.

"Your lions are miserable," she said.

"I know," sighed Bill.

"Your penguins are terrified."

"I know," said Bill. "They are losing their feathers and I don't know what to do about it."

"I do," said Gwenda. "What's more, I know your lady panda is eating too much and your male not enough."

"You're right," said Bill. "There is such sadness in my zoo."

"You're not helping it," said Gwenda.

Bill looked down at this little squirt of a girl. How does she know these things, he wondered. But he also had a feeling that he should not ask or argue.

"Gwenda, I have problems. The man who owns the zoo wants to make more money."

"He won't make more money if his animals are unhappy," replied Gwenda. "His animals will not have babies, they'll lose their feathers, they'll starve to death. Then he won't make any money at all."

"I know you're right," said Bill, quietly.

30

"How would you like to be them? Put yourself in their cages for a few days. You'd soon see, and Bill, it's up to you, no one else can or will help. I'm sure we can come up with nicer tricks to make money for your zoo, but first you must promise me you will always keep me and my words a secret."

"I promise," said Bill.

"And you must also help me out of a jam with my mother. Will you call her up and say you found me crying in the parking lot because the others had driven off without me?"

Gwenda told Bill her telephone number. He dialed it and spoke to her mother.

"I'm glad I called. She was beginning to get worried. She's on her way and she's very relieved," said Bill.

"Now please let me talk, and you listen, Bill," said Gwenda. "Did you take away Zelda's cubs?"

"Yes," said Bill, looking guilty.

"Do you make your penguins parade for their supper?"

"Yes, I'm afraid I do."

"Do you make them turn right by the wolves and do they always try to turn left?"

"Yes," gasped Bill, amazed.

"Well, you should have thought about it more," said

31

Gwenda. "It's your job to think for the animals. Did you put the lady panda straight into the panda cage without giving them time to get to know each other slowly?"

"But it's money, Gwenda. It's money and time. Mr. Mollyskin, the man who owns the zoo, wanted the pandas to hurry and have babies to draw the crowds. He wanted to make the penguins parade to make people laugh. He made me take Zelda's cubs to the children's zoo, so we could get more people in to watch them being bottle-fed."

"Okay, Bill, but we can change it. I know we can. The animals love you—you are the only person they have to protect them, so they need you more than Mr. Mollyskin does. We'll keep Mr. Mollyskin happy, but your job is to protect your animals."

While Bill made Gwenda a mug of cocoa and a huge cheese sandwich, Gwenda told Bill why his pandas were not having babies. She told him that the penguins lived in fear, and how to change it. She warned him of Zelda's deep unhappiness and how he must give the lion cubs back to Zimba and Zelda.

Bill never asked Gwenda how she knew these things. He knew better.

"I promise you, Gwenda, tomorrow I'll change it, I'll change it all."

"Now, here's my idea. Mr. Mollyskin will like it," said Gwenda. "It's a corker."

As Gwenda munched away at her enormous sandwich, she told Bill of a way the zoo could make lots of money.

"You build a cage, an empty cage. Then you put a sign at the front of the zoo saying that the zoo expects people to treat the animals kindly and respect them. Anyone found being cruel or making fun of the animals will have the same thing done to them. Then you make sure that the keepers guard the animals, and the minute you catch an idiot being nasty you stick him straight in the special cage. It will work wonderfully. Gosh, on Sundays and holidays the cages will be packed. Then other people will come to see and make fun of the bullies. The zoo will be crammed with happy animals and with any luck people will end up making fun of people."

"Mr. Mollyskin will love the idea," shouted Bill. "Hurrah, you're a magician."

Gwenda smiled, and as she did Bill swore he could hear the magical sound of a huge bird flapping its wings, and he saw flashes of light like sparklers come from Gwenda's eyes.

Nowadays, Uncle Matt does not go to the zoo. He did

not enjoy his last visit, when he found himself in a cage with a crowd of people laughing at him and the monkeys in the cage opposite copying his every move.

But Gwenda goes to the zoo a lot. She often gets a telephone call from Bill, usually asking her to visit and solve a problem.

"Gwenda," he says, "I think we need advice."

And Gwenda always goes in when the crowds have gone home. She chats to Zelda and Zimba and their family, gossips with the penguins, admires the pandas' baby; and all her animal friends share their worries with her. Even the wolves have stopped calling her "Little Red Riding Hood," and try to be polite when she passes.

If there's a problem that Bill has missed, the bats always lead her to it.

When she's finished her rounds, Gwenda knocks on Bill's door. Together they sit while Gwenda eats a huge cheese sandwich with a mug of cocoa, and they talk about the animals.